THIS MEANS YOU.

A S T E S.

3

DO YOU LIKE CATS?

(HEY ARE NOT FOR EVERYBODY.)

4

DO YOU LIKE BEING TICKLED?

WHICH IS 7 BETTER, MONSTERS OR DINOSAURS?

8 WHICH IS BETTER, SWIMMIN OR DANC

In memory of Rob Moss, who liked jazz, classical literature, beautiful women, and telling stories. I don't know what his favorite thing was—but I hope he's got a lot of it, now.   —E. J.

Giorgio + Daddy + Mummy + Roberta + James + Romeo + Eolo = My Favorite Family!!!   —A. C.

Atheneum Books for Young Readers
An imprint of Simon & Schuster
Children's Publishing Division
1230 Avenue of the Americas
New York, New York 10020

Text copyright © 2004 by Emily Jenkins

Illustrations copyright © 2004 by AnnaLaura Cantone

Book design by Lee Wade. The text for this book is set in Barbera.

Manufactured in China

First Edition

10 9 8 7 6 5 4 3 2 1

Library of Congress Cataloging-in-Publication Data

Jenkins, Emily, 1967-

My favorite thing / Emily Jenkins ; illustrated by AnnaLaura Cantone.— 1st ed.   p. cm.

"An Anne Schwartz Book."

Summary: In words and pictures, Alberta shares what she likes and does not like about dogs, cats, baths, and many other things as she leads up to what she likes best of all.

ISBN 0-689-84975-3

[1. Individuality—Fiction.] I. Cantone, Anna-Laura, ill. II. Title.

PZ7.J4134My 2004

[E]—dc21

2002155258

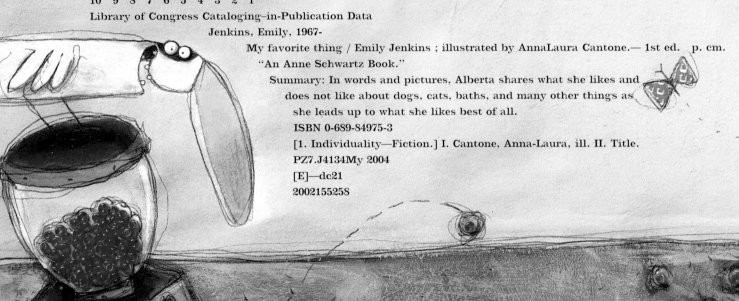

MY FAVORITE THING

(ACCORDING TO ALBERTA)

Emily Jenkins

ILLUSTRATED BY AnnaLaura Cantone

AN ANNE SCHWARTZ BOOK

Atheneum Books for Young Readers

New York   London   Toronto   Sydney

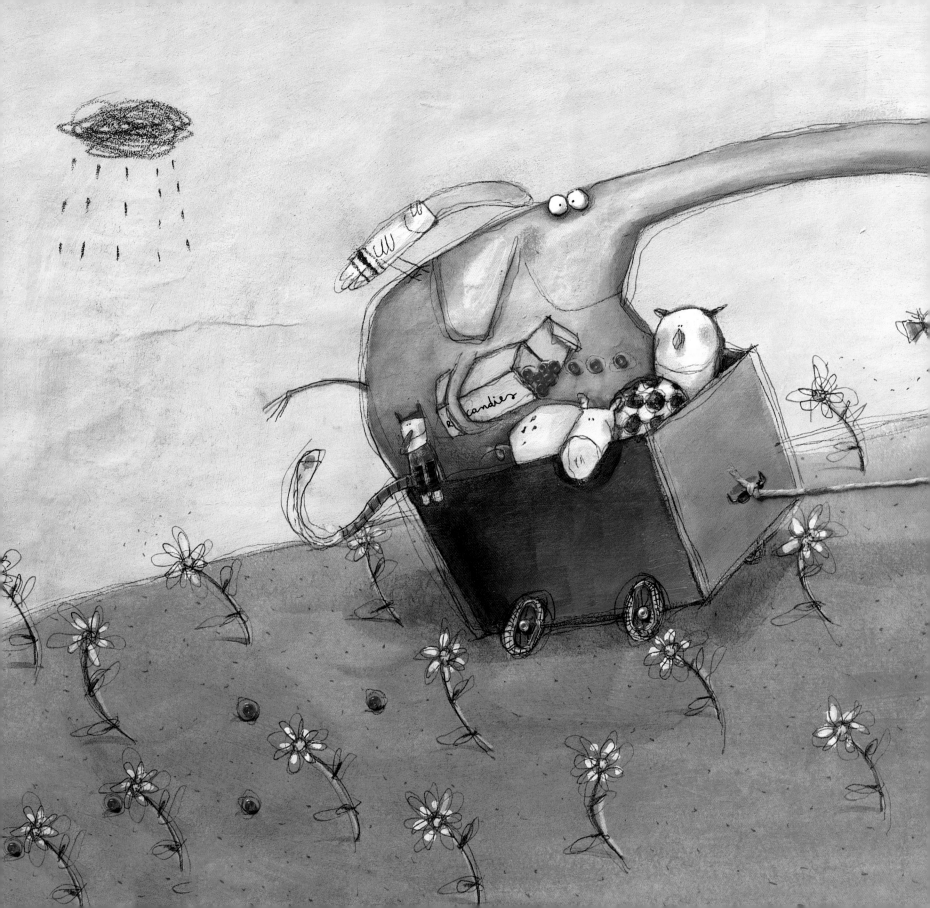

Alberta is a girl

of particular

tastes.

Dogs are not
her favorite thing.

BAD

BETTER

"I do not like large ones that drool, but small ones that keep their tongues in their mouths are okay," explains Alberta. "Dogs have to be smaller than my knee for me to like them."

BEST

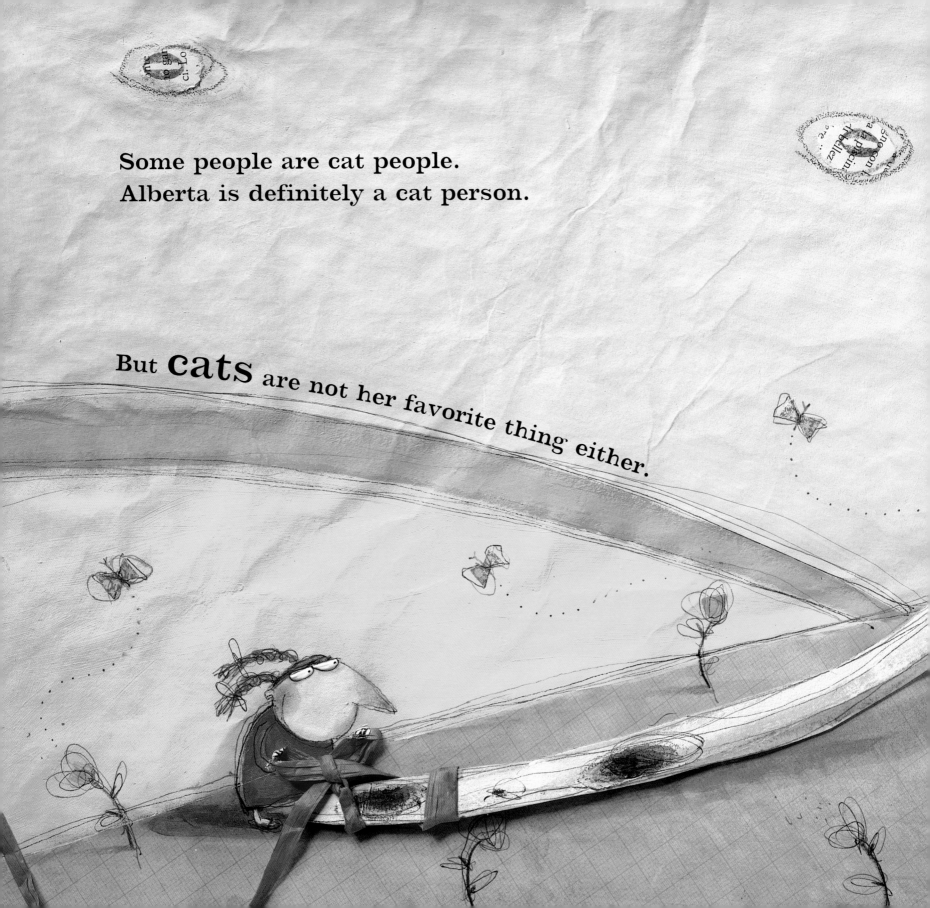

Some people are cat people.
Alberta is definitely a cat person.

But cats are not her favorite thing either.

Not
even her
own cat,
whose name is
NepTUnE.

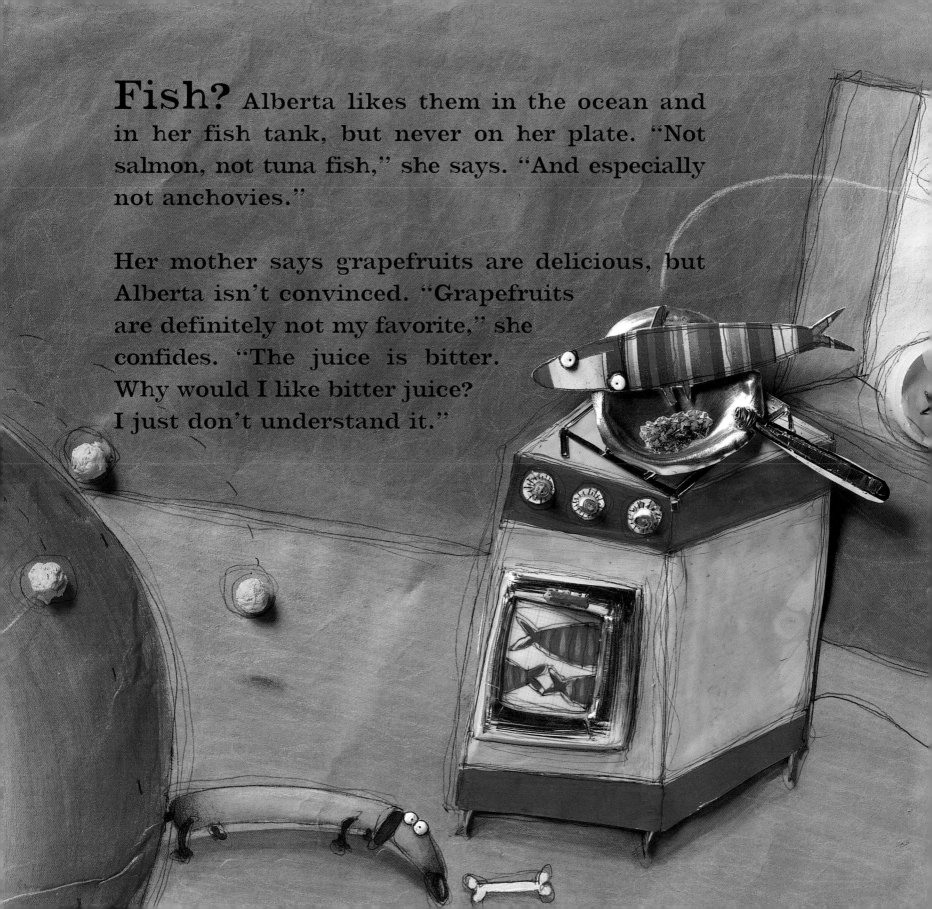

Fish? Alberta likes them in the ocean and in her fish tank, but never on her plate. "Not salmon, not tuna fish," she says. "And especially not anchovies."

Her mother says grapefruits are delicious, but Alberta isn't convinced. "Grapefruits are definitely not my favorite," she confides. "The juice is bitter. Why would I like bitter juice? I just don't understand it."

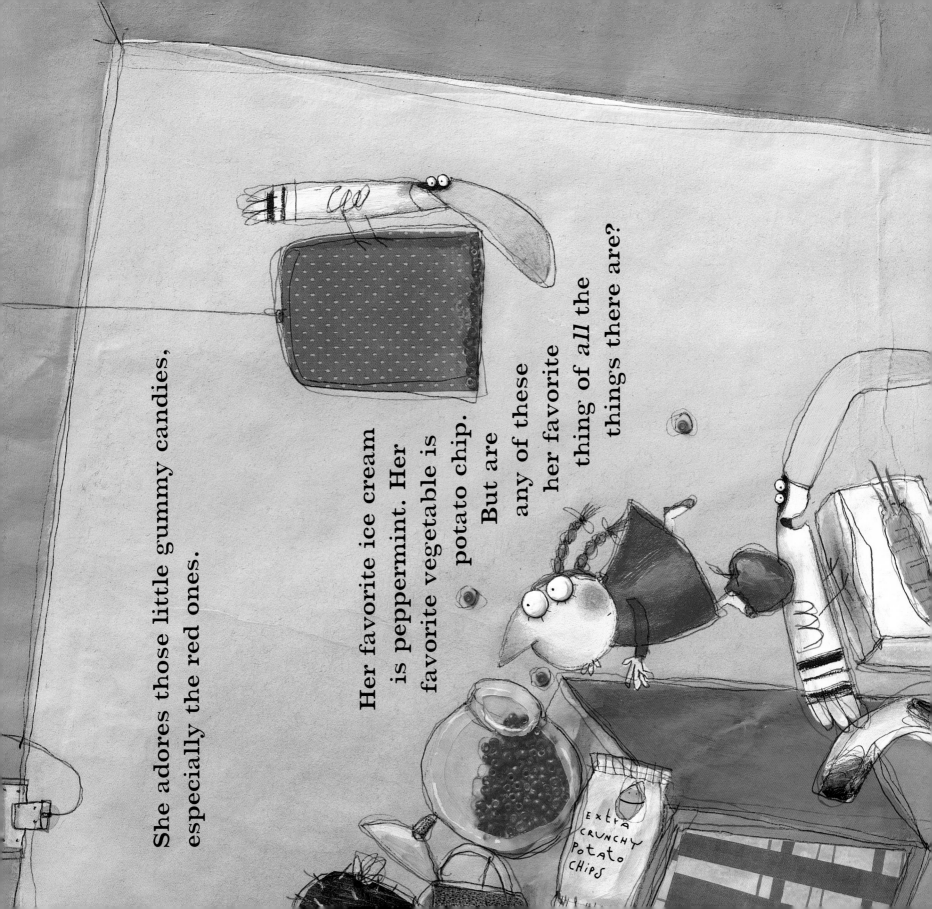

She adores those little gummy candies, especially the red ones.

Her favorite ice cream is peppermint. Her favorite vegetable is potato chip. But are any of these her favorite thing of all the things there are?

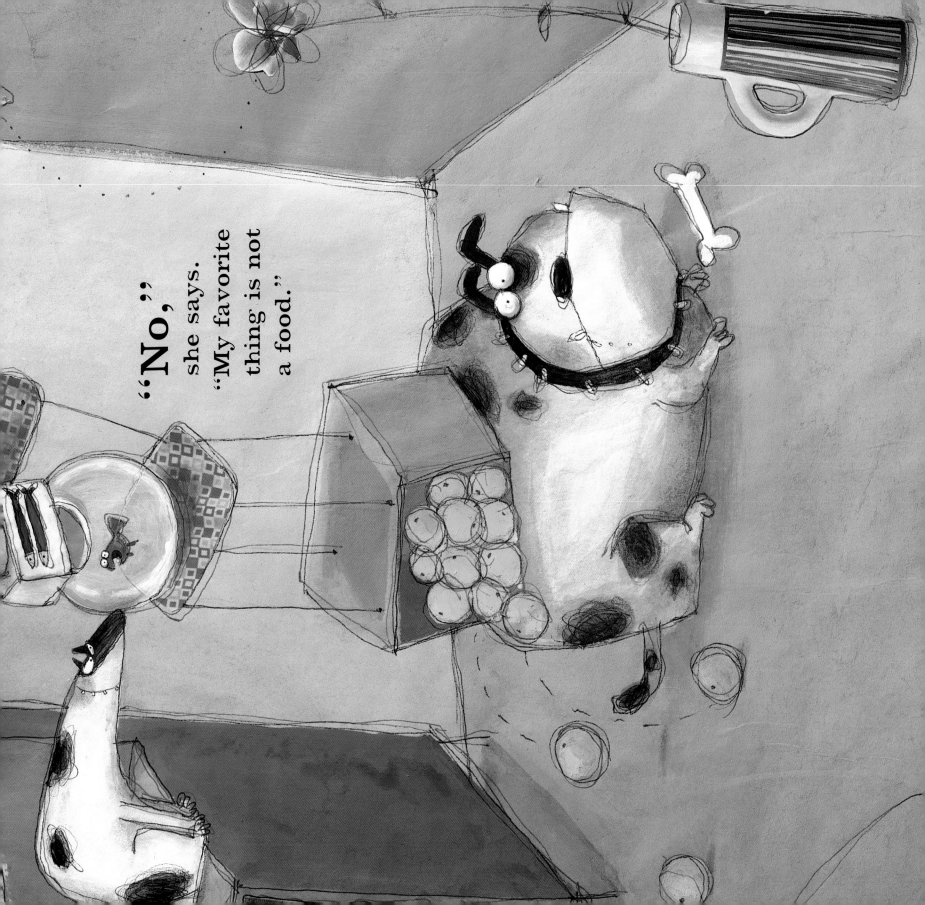

"No," she says. "My favorite thing is not a food."

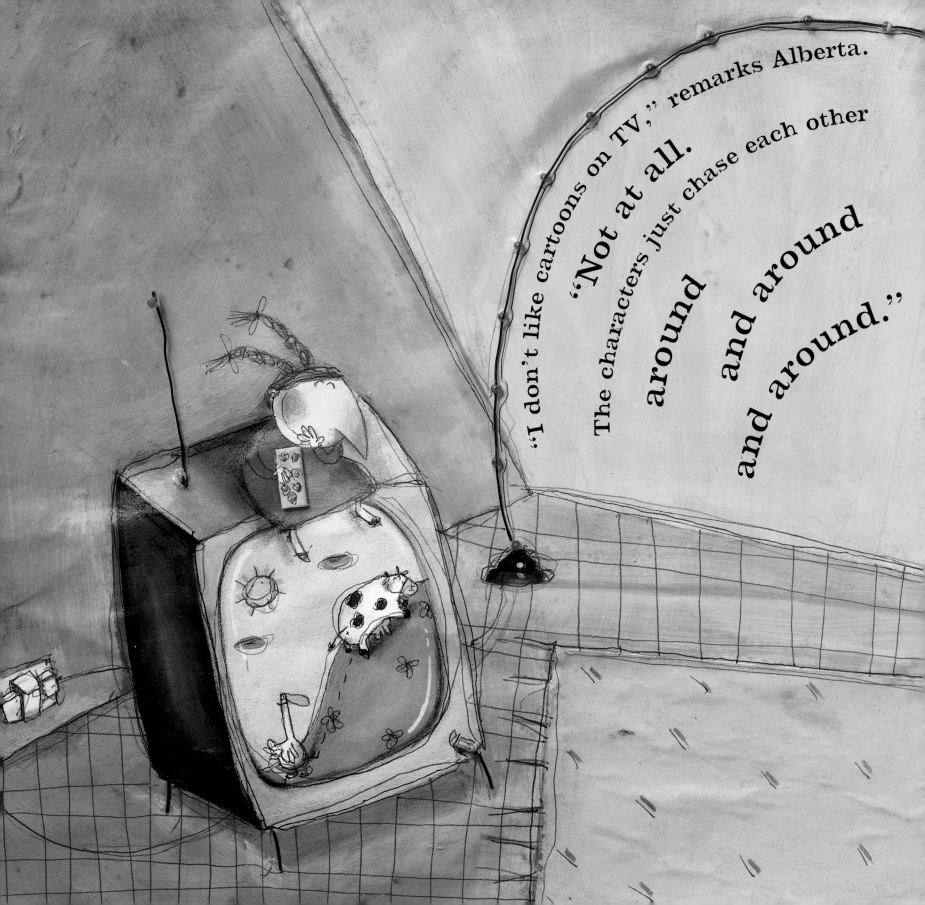

"I don't like cartoons on TV," remarks Alberta. "Not at all. The characters just chase each other around and around and around."

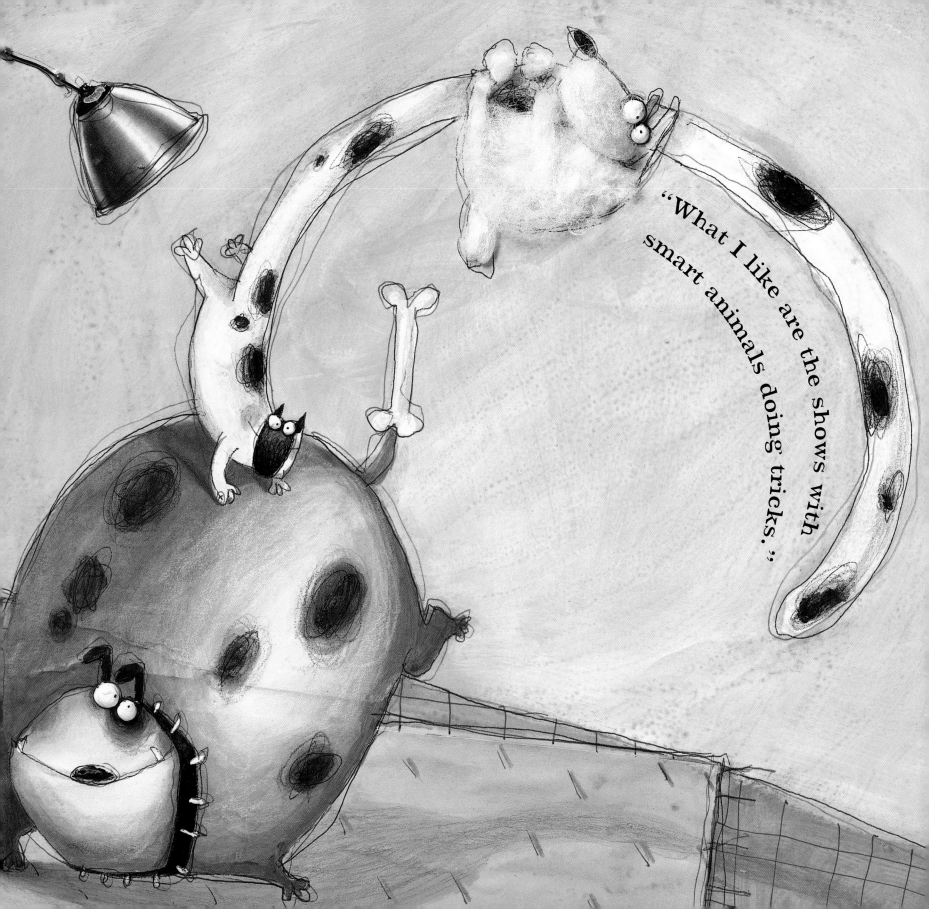

"What I like are the shows with smart animals doing tricks."

WHAT DO A SPIDER AND
A GRAPE HAVE
IN COMMON?
BOTH HAVE
8 LEGS,
EXCEPT FOR THE
GRAPE.

Then there's her brother, Marshall. "I like him *some* of the time," says Alberta.

"He can touch his nose with his tongue and knows a lot of riddles.

"But when he tells me I'm too young to play with him and his stupid nine-year-old friends, then I don't like him one bit."

Alberta's favorite color is orange, because anything that's orange looks terrifically exciting.

But a color isn't really the sort of thing that's a favorite out of all the things there are to like.

Lots of people don't appreciate baths, but Alberta likes to soak in the tub for hours. "I stay until my feet look prune-y," she says. "I have three rubber sharks."

Are baths her favorite thing, then?
"No," says Alberta. "Not baths."

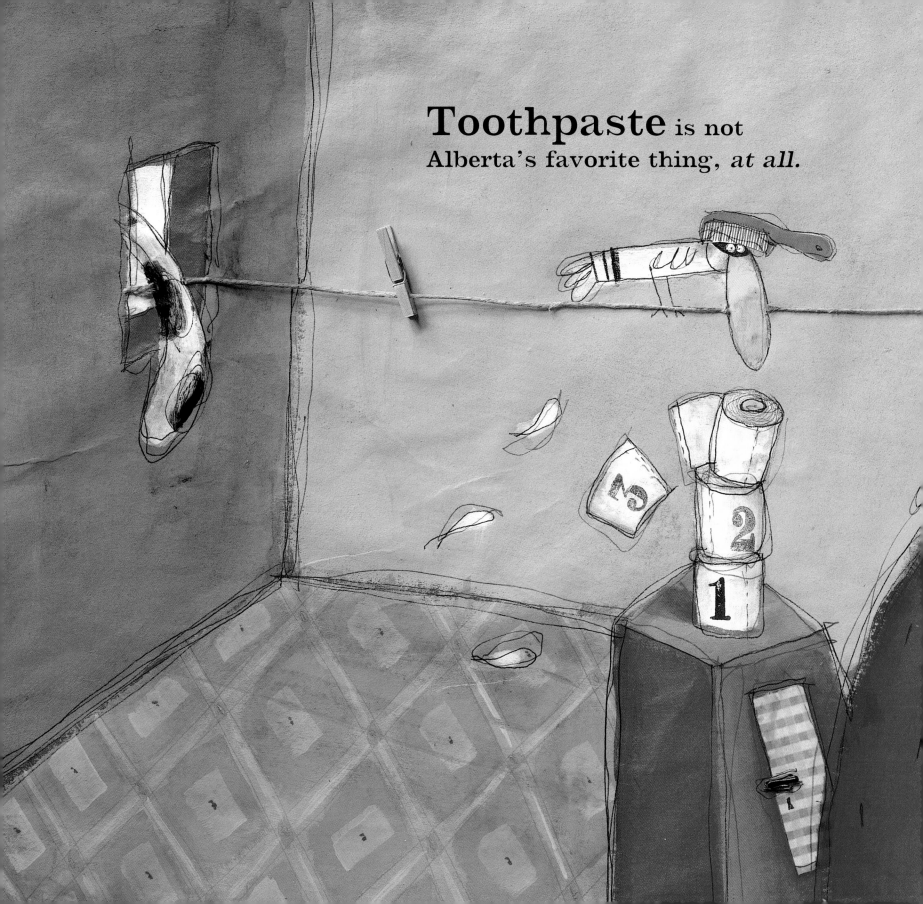

Toothpaste is not
Alberta's favorite thing, *at all.*

She has tried mint, cherry, orange, and bubble-gum flavor, but none of them tastes very good. "If I could never brush my teeth ever again, that would be fine with me."

"Know what I love?" asks Alberta.

"Boats!"

She hasn't been on a very big one,
though, like a yacht or an aircraft carrier.
  She has been in a canoe.
  Also, a rubber raft.
  So, are boats her favorite thing?
  Nope, not boats.

Here is something Alberta does not like: baby dolls. "They seem as if they might come to life in the middle of the night and attack," she says.

What she likes instead are stuffed owls, because owls can see in the dark and keep watch over her sleep.

There are eight of them living on her bed. The littlest one is missing an eye.

Alberta likes what she likes.
Where does it come from?

She isn't sure.

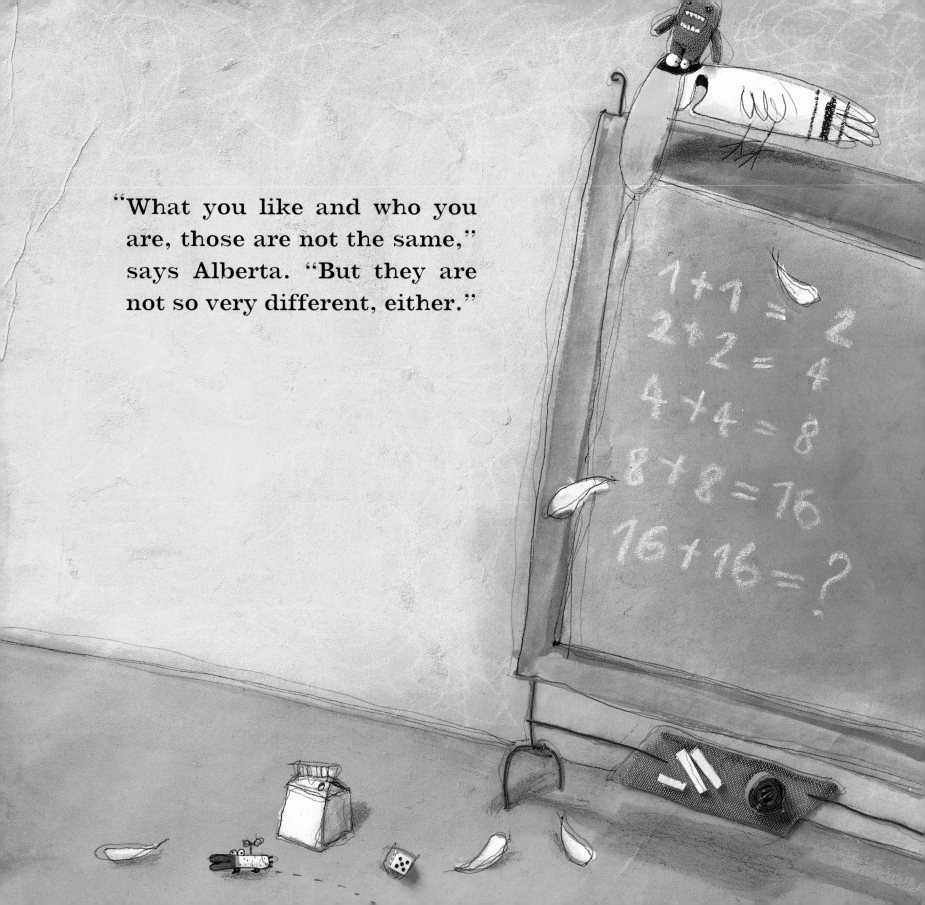

"What you like and who you are, those are not the same," says Alberta. "But they are not so very different, either."

$1 + 1 = 2$
$2 + 2 = 4$
$4 + 4 = 8$
$8 + 8 = 16$
$16 + 16 = ?$

So, wouldn't you like to know Alberta's favorite thing?
What could it be, her favorite thing?
"That's easy," says Alberta, the girl with particular tastes.

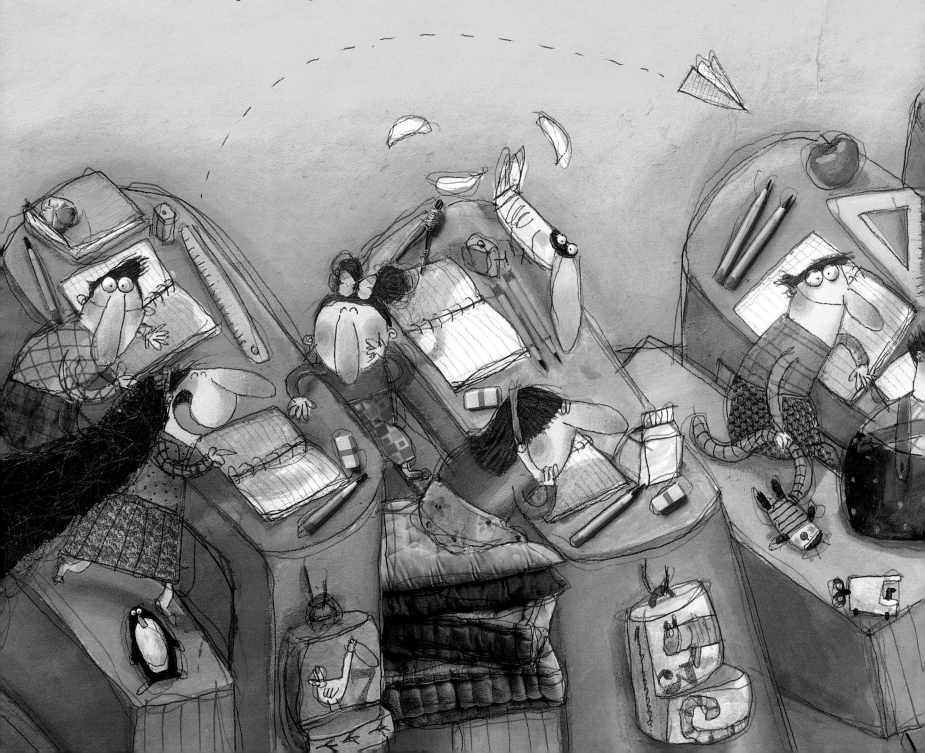

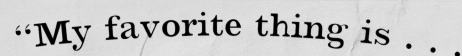

"My favorite thing is . . .

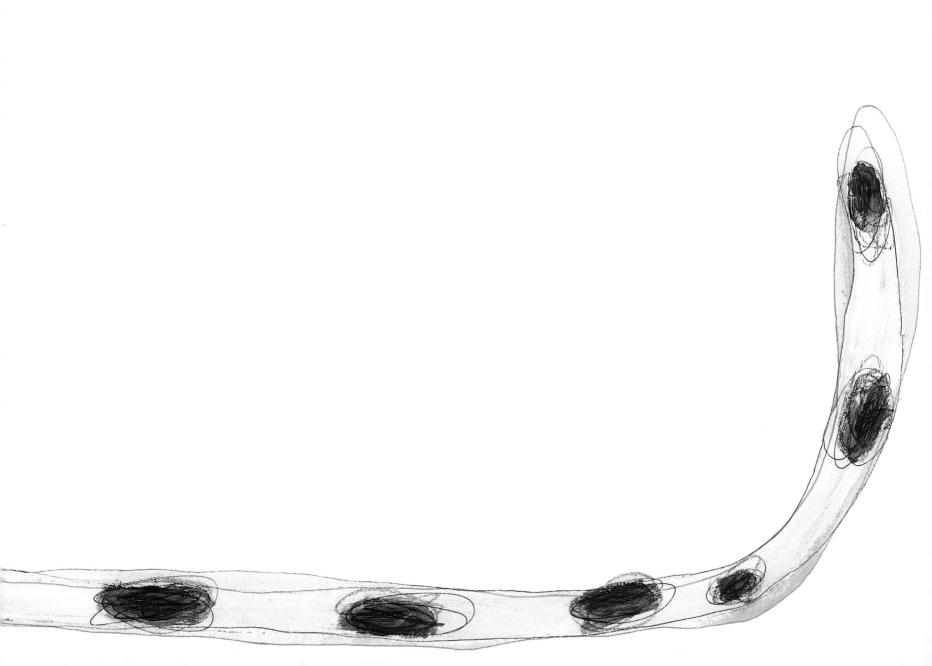

EVERYONE HAS 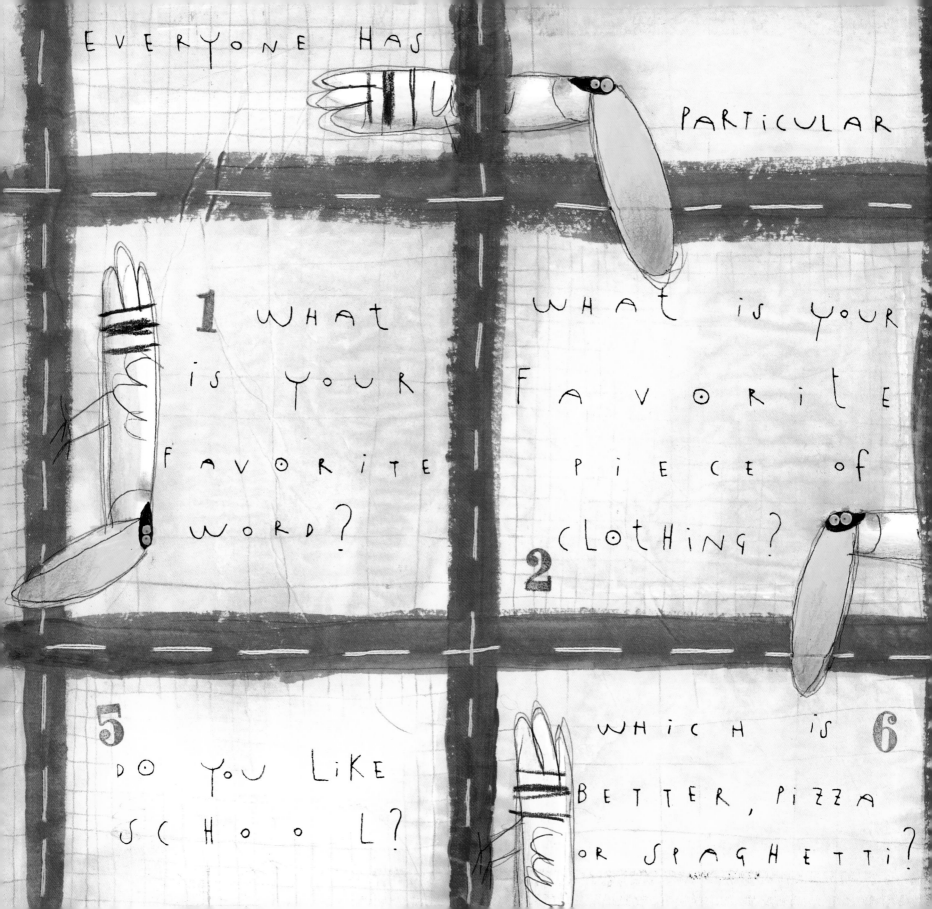 PARTICULAR

1 WHAT is YOUR FAVORITE WORD?

WHAT is YOUR FAVORITE PIECE of CLOTHING? 2

5 DO YOU LIKE SCHOOL?

WHICH is 6 BETTER, PIZZA OR SPAGHETTI?